A TRIP TO MARS

ARCHEOASTRONAUTICS

FRANCIS A. ANDREW

Order this book online at www.trafford.com
or email orders@trafford.com

Most Trafford titles are also available at major online book retailers.

Print information available on the last page.

ISBN: 978-1-4907-9446-4 (sc)
ISBN: 978-1-4907-9445-7 (hc)
ISBN: 978-1-4907-9447-1 (e)

Library of Congress Control Number: 2019903521

Trafford rev. 03/26/2019

www.trafford.com
North America & international
toll-free: 1 888 232 4444 (USA & Canada)
fax: 812 355 4082

Dedication

I dedicate this book to the late Mrs. Mary Hopkins who died in 2018. Without Mary's inspiration, I would never have embarked upon the writing and publication of books. May her soul rest in peace.

CONTENTS

FOREWORD

"It is now fifty years since the first Moon landing took place and Neil Armstrong uttered those unforgettable words, etched on the memories of not only those who witnessed the event but on the collective consciousness of all mankind throughout all ages thereafter - "that's one small step for a man, one giant leap for mankind." Fifty years on and mankind, far from attaining the goal of a manned mission to Mars, has not yet returned to Earth's nearest neighbour - the Moon. Andrew's novel has therefore come at a most crucial time in the history of space travel. Through having two of his characters, Harry Holbert and Margaret Woodford, coining a new word - "archeoastronautics," which involves the recovery of old astronautical technology, Francis Andrew's novel comes as a clarion call to space travel enthusiasts, professional and amateur alike, to move forward with renewed enthusiasm for the conquest of space." Yatender (Yashu) Singh. Delhi, India.

CHAPTER I

THE ORBITING CITY

Mars Endeavour had been under construction for ten years. It was a "city" one mile in diameter and one hundred feet in height. The most interesting thing about *Mars Endeavour* was that it was built in a one-thousand-mile orbit above the Earth. Its mission was to fly to Mars as part of a major project that NASA had been engaged in for twenty years—to colonize the Red Planet. From 2034 to 2054, NASA had been sending spacecraft to Mars with materials and supplies necessary for human beings to live there.

It all turned out to be an amazing feat of technology. Along with the supplies, armies of robots were released onto the surface of the Red Planet. They had been preprogrammed to assemble the materials into one huge city. Their actions were controlled by NASA scientists and computers on Earth. The site chosen was close to the Vallis Marineris, a huge Grand Canyon-type structure running for 2,485 miles along the Martian equator. Vast deposits of underground water had been discovered in the Vallis Marineris, so this essential resource would be a major boost for future colonists of Mars.

The robots had laid the basis of the model city upon which all future Martian cities would be constructed. The city measured three miles by three miles. Outside of it was a huge nuclear generator for the supply of energy to the city, namely light and heat. It was planned that the city would be home to eventually one thousand people; mainly scientists looking for a bit of adventure, young people willing to "tough it out" on the Red Planet for at least a couple of decades of their lives, and some might even want to make Mars their permanent home. The city consisted of houses and streets, parks and play areas, gymnasia, cinemas, theaters—well, almost anything you would find in a terrestrial city. But it was all under a dome, a massive dome to protect its inhabitants from the severe cold of Mars, dangerous radiation (Mars has no magnetic field and only a thin atmosphere) from outer space, and possible meteor strikes. The model Martian city, considering the massive dome covering it, was aptly named Dome City.

One of the major problems for the Mars city planners had been from where to obtain the cities' oxygen supplies. However, during a school trip to NASA, one smart girl mentioned a book she had read concerning that. The book was titled *Peril on Mars*. It had been written as far back as 1958 by Sir Patrick Moore. Moore had envisioned growing on Mars forests of oxygen-yielding plants. These plants, when plucked, would be taken inside a dome-type structure where their oxygen would be released.

Although the girl's suggestion was initially dismissed by scientists, one bio-engineer, Dr. Jeremy Flockston, who had just finished his doctoral studies, was stimulated by what he had heard from the young girl. He got hold of Moore's *Peril on Mars* and, after reading it, was further motivated into using Sir Patrick Moore's basic idea and painstakingly got down to work on genetically modifying plants that could perform the function of giving off copious amounts of oxygen. In cooperation with NASA's planetary engineers, Flockston designed an industrial process to channel the oxygen from a power-producing factory to the city. "Moore's Plants," as they eventually came to be known, when fully grown, were to be plucked and taken from the forests to the factory where, when undergoing a crushing process, would release their stores of oxygen. This oxygen would then be released through a series of funnels to the city. A full-scale model of this industrial process had shown its complete workability. Further research and development carried out by Dr. Flockston and his team had created an improved sub-species of the plant which enabled it to reproduce and grow rapidly, such rapid reproduction and growth being essential to meet the oxygen demands of an expanding Martian population.

Near the Vallis Marineris, the robots had constructed machinery to drill down to the water deposits. Massive pumps would be used to bring the water to the surface and store it in large water tanks from where it would be distributed to the Martians living in Dome City.

The purpose of *Mars Endeavour* in all this was to fly to Mars with six crew members who were to activate the life-support systems of Dome City. They were to implement the finishing touches to the nuclear generator, the plant-crushing equipment, and the water-pumping machinery. It would take about a year to have all the machinery in motion and, thus, Dome City to be fully habitable. During this time, *Mars Endeavour* would be home to the six crew members. Once Dome City was fully functional, *Mars Endeavour* would be incorporated into it as a "suburb."

Maurice Cuthbertson, the NASA administrator, was giving a final briefing to the crew prior to their departure.

"Well," said Cuthbertson, "everything seems to be just tickety boo. We've checked the robots, and they are all in good working order. According to the system we have set up, they will be controlled by you guys but with backup from Mission Control here at NASA if required. Tomorrow morning, the shuttle will take you to *Mars Endeavour*, and three hours later, you will activate all systems and be on your way to Mars. Anyway, the press are here. Let's all go out to the press briefing hall and answer some of their questions."

Cuthbertson and the six crew members made their way from the administrator's plush office to the press briefing hall, which was all abuzz with reporters eager for information about the grand finale to this amazing Mars project.

"Hi! I'm Stan Brookson from the *New York Times*. I'd like to ask the captain of *Mars Endeavour* how long he and his crew will be away from Earth for."

"Well, Mr. Brookson," said Capt. Joseph Blackwood, "first of all, thank you for your question. It will take us only six months to get to Mars using the nuclear-powered engines of *Mars Endeavour*.

We shall then spend two years on Mars. The first year will be spent getting all the life-support systems functioning, and the second year will be spent conducting experiments and carrying out explorations of the surrounding area."

"Sheila Witherton from the *Washington Post*—are you confident your oxygen supplies will be sufficient for that period of time?"

"We have supplies on *Mars Endeavour* for three years. That covers the six-month flight to the planet and the two years we'll be there plus six months extra for good measure. However, once the machinery for obtaining oxygen from the plants is fully operational, we'll be self-sufficient in oxygen."

"What about food supplies?" asked a *Time* reporter.

"I think my colleague, Dr. Jeremy Flockston, who is a bio-engineer, can best answer that question."

"Thank you, Joseph," said Jeremy. "We have sufficient food for three years on *Mars Endeavour*. For future supplies, the robots have constructed a farming facility under a dome two miles in diameter. The mission which will follow us in two years will bring cows, sheep, pigs, goats, poultry, and fish and a great variety of vegetable seeds. We reckon that within five years from then, the Martian colonies will be self-sufficient in food."

"Chris Walters from the *Chicago Daily*—how do you plan to return to Earth?"

"Rodney! Could you take this one?" said Joseph.

Rodney Roberts, a rocket engineer, explained how this would be done. "The assemblages for a return craft are already on Mars. My job will be, along with the robots, to assemble these pieces into a fully-functioning craft to take my colleagues and I safely back to Earth."

"Marie Matthews from the *Boston Globe*—will you be conducting any science experiments that benefit humanity?"

"Georgina Trombers is an astronomer," replied Joseph. "She will tell you about her role in the Mars mission."

"Some of the assemblage parts already transported to Mars," began Georgina, "will be constructed into a three-hundred-inch reflecting telescope. The thin atmosphere on Mars will give astronomers a much clearer picture of the universe."

"Heather Wilber is a physicist," said Joseph. "She will now explain what she will be doing on Mars."

"Initially, we will construct a kind of mini version of the Large Hadron Collider to study fundamental particles of matter in a low-gravity environment," said Heather. "However, we have an ambitious program, which is to transport enough parts to assemble a construction twice as large as the LHC. We are certain to discover many more fundamental particles of matter and transform physics as we currently know it."

After some more questions, Maurice Cuthbertson ended the press conference and the crew members went out of the hall.

CHAPTER

II

FARE THEE WELL, EARTH

The six crew members entered the shuttle that would ferry them to *Mars Endeavour*, the floating city that would be their home for the next three years. They had mixed feelings about their trip. Their thoughts flitted between wondering what it would be like to be 140 million miles away from the Earth for three years and the excitement of the great adventure which lay before them. Though they were being jostled by a plethora of mental images rushing in and out of their heads, their rigorous training had ensured that their faces were emotionless as they strapped themselves into their seats in the shuttle, readying themselves for takeoff.

At last, the engines of the shuttle were activated, and the crew felt the craft lifting off from the Earth. Up, up, and up they went. Soon they were feeling the intense pressure on their bodies as the craft fought against the Earth's gravitational pull, whose escape velocity is eight miles per second. When they were free of Earth's gravity, the worst was over, and they could relax. They looked out of the craft's porthole-type windows and saw the massive orbiting city shimmering in the sunlight against the blackness of space. The closer they approached, the bigger it appeared. And the bigger it appeared, the less apprehensive they were about this being their home for almost three years. Yet they still had reservations about living in this vast metal contraption.

"I find it hard to imagine that that metal monster resembles an average-sized terrestrial town with all the facilities and amenities that such a town would normally have," commented Heather.

"Don't judge a book by its cover," replied Joseph in mildly scolding tones.

"Once we're inside," said Jeremy, "it will look quite different."

"We'll probably even forget we've left the Earth," said Georgina with a chuckle.

"Just . . . let's all make the best of it," said Rodney somewhat dryly.

"Just think of it," said James, "we have a city all to ourselves. The fact that there are only six of us in this one-mile-square city will make it seem even bigger than it already is. Think of it—no crowds, no pollution from fossil-fuel-burning vehicles, no factories belching out smoke and fumes, no traffic jams on the roads, no criminals waiting to rob you or mug you at the next street corner, no waiting in queues . . . oh, and so much more!"

When they reached the gigantic structure which would be their home for the next three years, the shuttle started slowing as it approached the docking area. The amazing thing about the shuttle was that it was pilotless; it was guided by Mission

Control at Houston back on Earth. After waiting a few minutes, the massive door of *Mars Endeavour*'s docking area started moving upward. Guided by Mission Control and its computer programming system, the shuttle slowly moved into *Mars Endeavour*. After the docking area was pressurized, the shuttle door opened, and the crew disembarked. When they left the docking area, the shuttle returned to Earth.

"Blackwood to Mission Control," said Joseph as he radioed back to NASA, "we have successfully embarked and are now on the control deck."

"Roger," came a voice. "Activate forward movement." Joseph, like Rodney, was a rocket scientist. They both put *Mars Endeavour* into operating mode and waited for the onboard computer system to start up the nuclear-powered engines on the massive craft. Twenty five of these engines were placed around the exterior of the craft.

The gigantic structure, at first, moved at a slow-ish speed, one that would get them past the moon in about thirty-six hours. Once past the moon, *Mars Endeavour* would go at full speed toward the Red Planet.

Joseph and his team then spent hours walking around the massive city. They strolled through its parks and gardens and had their meal in one of the plush restaurants. Everything was automatic. An electronic menu was presented by a robot. Each crew member indicated his/her preference by touchscreen. Twenty or so minutes later, the robots returned with the dishes cooked and prepared by robotic chefs in a fully-automated kitchen.

When dinner was over, the waiter robots cleared away the dishes and took them back to the kitchen, where dishwashing robots cleaned the plates, bowls, and cups and efficiently stacked them away. All the robots then went into sleeping mode.

Each crew member was allotted a detached villa-type residence. These also had their robots: robots to cook and clean, robots to attend to the garden, robots to put out and recycle the trash, even robots to play board games with.

At the gym, there were robot trainers. In the parks, there were robot ice cream vendors. In the cinemas, robot ushers were there to show members of the audience to their seats. Almost every film that had ever been made was available through the compressed digitized forms on which they were stored. Robotized taxis were available everywhere to drive the crew members to different parts of the city.

The museums and art galleries were digitally connected to those on Earth. By selecting one, a virtual world opened up, whereby the "visitor" could "walk" around, say, the Louvre, the Smithsonian, or London's Natural History Museum and be given an explanation of the artifacts by a virtual guide.

"This is what the Garden of Eden must have looked like," said Jeremy. "As a biological engineer, I would love to examine the flora and fauna of that original paradise."

"It's just a myth," commented Rodney in his usual dull matter-of-fact tones.

"That's what I thought until I saw this," said Heather.

"As you all know," said Joseph, "we all have work to do. So it won't be all gadding about in a paradise of pleasure."

The main job of the crew members for the next six months would be to ensure that their equipment was ready for assemblage on Mars: James' mining gear, Jeremy's seedlings and embryos in suspended animation, Rodney's rocket templates and rocket-making programming for the robots, Georgina's astronomical equipment, and Heather's mini LHC.

CHAPTER

III

"HOUSTON, WE HAVE A PROBLEM."

Although Georgina Trombers was an astronomer, her interests extended into other areas of science. Her main task on Mars was to set up optical, radio, and spectroscopic equipment to study the universe in low gravitational and thin atmospheric conditions. One thing that greatly fascinated her was the field of astrobiology. After reading *Diseases from Space* (Hoyle and Wickramasinghe, 1979), Georgina studied astrobiology in her free time and read as much literature as she could get hold of on it.

"One of the questions I'm often asked when discussing the issue of bacteria and viruses originating from space and their being the building blocks of evolution on planets is as to how these pathogens actually form," said Georgina to Heather Wilber and Jeremy Flockston when they were sitting in a cafeteria one "day" sipping on cappuccinos. Joseph had insisted that he and his fellow crew members stick to a terrestrial twenty-four-hour day so as to ensure that their bodies did not get out of kilter with their biological rhythms.

"It seems that after so much spectroscopic work on interstellar gas clouds, it is quite clear that bacteria and viruses are space incident," replied Jeremy.

"I am sure that bacterial spores are formed during supernova explosions," said Georgina thoughtfully.

"But the principle laid down by Louis Pasteur in the nineteenth century and accepted to this day is that life can only come from life."

"Yes," replied Georgina, "and that is true regarding the replication of life under tranquil conditions and once it has developed from its base beginnings. But what are those base beginnings? Such has never been observed under normal and tranquil conditions."

"So you are suggesting that life's origins are to be found under—eh, let us say 'abnormal conditions.'"

"Indeed. It is also important to note that the Pasteurian principle is concerned with the replication of life and not with the origin of life—a distinction that should be well understood."

"Well," said James Skelton, who had overheard much of the conversation when he was instructing the robot on what food and beverages to bring him, "I'm a simple miner by trade, but in my mining experiences on Earth, I've seen fossilized single-celled life in the rocks I have examined. Magnification of these rocks show fossilized bacteria almost four billion years old. Now considering that the Earth formed 4.5 billion years ago, it would seem that the origin and development of life on our planet was more or less coterminous with its geological origin and development." James sat himself down with Heather, Jeremy, and Georgina. At length, the robot came and brought James his coffee and cheese-and-ham sandwich.

"I think we could advance the science of astrobiology if we all worked together," said Georgina. "Hoyle and Wickramasinghe repeatedly emphasized the interdisciplinary nature of astrobiology," continued Georgina.

It was at this point that their deliberations on astrobiology were rudely interrupted by the *Mars Endeavour*'s alarm system sounding. "Would everyone come immediately to the control room?" came the somber voice of Rodney Roberts over the craft's loud-speaker systems. The four of them looked at one another in surprise and wondered what all this could be about. They commented that it might be just a routine practice drill.

When they entered the control room, they were confronted with an ashen-faced Rodney Roberts. "There is a major fault in our nuclear-powered engines," said Rodney. "I have made a thorough examination of the systems and have to announce to you honestly that we cannot continue on to Mars." Looks of alarm and disbelief came over the faces of his colleagues.

"Have you informed Mission Control in Houston about this?" asked Joseph.

"I have," replied Rodney, "and their conclusion is the same as mine. We cannot proceed to Mars. As you are also a rocket scientist like myself," continued Rodney, "you might also like to make an inspection of the engines and give us your take on it."

In his capacity as captain and rocket engineer, Joseph Blackwood proceeded to check the craft's engines. Half an hour later, he reentered the control room grimly concurring with Rodney's analysis.

"So can we return to Earth?" Georgina asked.

Joseph and Rodney looked seriously at each other and gravely shook their heads in reply.

"Do you mean that we are stranded here in space forever?" said Heather, displaying a lot of panic in her voice.

"Let me get in touch with Houston again for a further analysis and plan of action," suggested Rodney. Joseph nodded in consent. It was around twenty minutes later that Rodney faced his fellow crew members. "The situation is this," he began. "We are nearer to the moon than we are to Earth. Therefore, while we do not have enough power and thrust to return the craft to Earth, we must use what capacity we have left in the engines to continue toward the moon, use the moon's gravity to obtain extra stabilizing thrust for an orbit, and then select a suitable landing place for the craft."

Owing to the vastly-diminished power left in the craft's engines, it took two days before lunar orbit was achieved. During those two days, the crew made their plans for a safe-as-possible landing on the moon.

"How did this happen?" Jeremy Flockston asked Rodney.

"The matter is somewhat academic," replied Rodney, "the fact is it has happened, and we must do all we can to make the best of what remains of the craft."

"Was it a meteorite which perhaps ripped through a section of the craft?" inquired Georgina.

"I had thought of that," replied Rodney, "but I see no evidence of meteorite impact. The reason for such a malfunction on such a massive scale is beyond my imagining."

"The engines and their systems were thoroughly checked over and over again," said Joseph. "So I am at a complete loss as to how to account for our current circumstances."

CHAPTER
IV
LUNAR LANDING

A fter *Mars Endeavour* had made thirty orbits of the moon, Captain Blackwood had this announcement to make to the crew. "After having made long and meticulous calculations with Mission Control at Houston, we have decided to make our landing in the northern part of the Mare Tranquillitatis. Let us now return to our seats and prepare for landing."

Joseph and Rodney guided the craft down toward the lunar surface. Because of the damage that had been caused, the landing was rougher than had been expected. The two rocket engineers were thrown across the bridge of the control room on the craft's impact with the lunar surface. The other crew members, being strapped in their seats, were unaffected by the thrust caused by landing.

"Well, here we are on the lunar surface," said Jeremy. "What now?"

"There are a number of things we have to consider," said Joseph, "but first and foremost, we have to keep our nerve—that before anything else. Is that clear?" Heads were nodding in agreement.

"The most obvious question," said Heather Wilber, "is how we are going to get off the moon. The equipment, robotic backup, and materials for assembling the return craft are on Mars. We do not have these here with us."

"Rodney and I are aware of that," replied Joseph. "We have been in touch with Maurice Cuthbertson of NASA. And he will address us as soon as he has weighed up the situation."

"Captain Blackwood and I will make a complete check on the life-support systems of the craft," added Rodney in formalistic tones. "We will then report back to NASA. When Maurice has all the information, he will announce a plan of action."

Three hours later, Joseph Blackwood summoned the crew back to the control room. "Luckily, our life-support systems have not been damaged, though some of the robots have. But these can soon be repaired and put back into operation. I have sent a report back to Earth on our situation, and Maurice Cuthbertson, the NASA administrator, will assess things from a terrestrial viewpoint and inform us as to what action will be taken on NASA's part."

About three hours later, Maurice Cuthbertson's face appeared on the large screen. He looked tired and worn. He had this to say:

"Let me say to all of you that it has come as a great shock to me and all here at Mission Control in Houston, Texas, to learn of your predicament. It was not only my decision, but the unanimous verdict of all my colleagues here to recommend a lunar landing rather than a return to Earth given the severe damage to your craft's engines. Your captain and your rocket engineer also came to the same conclusion.

"It is vital, though, that we do not dwell upon the reasons for this most unexpectedly appalling mishap but rather consider a plan of action for the immediate and longer term. First of all, we suggest that, for the foreseeable future, you make the moon your base of operations. You are all highly qualified and experienced scientists, so we suggest that you use whatever equipment you have at your disposal to advance the cause of science, each in your own particular fields."

"What about a rescue plan?" cried out Georgina, interrupting Maurice's speech.

"I'm coming to that now," continued the administrator. "Unfortunately, we do not have the technology at our disposal to effect a rescue mission. The kind of craft that would have brought you back from Mars is designed to be a one-way journey. However, you have food and oxygen supplies for about three years."

"And after three years are up?" came the somber voice of Heather Wilber in serious interrogative tone.

"If we have still not designed a craft to rescue you by then, we can send unmanned craft to the moon with the necessary supplies for the support of life." And so Maurice continued in these conciliatory and reassuring tones for the next fifteen minutes before closing down the telecast.

"Well," said Joseph, "we have to get on with our lives as best we can. I am sure that NASA will make it top priority to design a craft to rescue us."

Over the next few weeks, the crew got down to their scientific duties. However, as most of the equipment was on Mars, they decided that they would have to ask NASA to ferry what they could to the moon. The members of the crew put in their requests to Joseph, who would then convey these to Maurice at Mission Control.

"The twenty-five-inch reflecting telescope we already have on board should be sufficient for me to carry out reasonably good astronomical work," said Georgina. "However, I would like the necessary parts sent for the construction of a spectroscope and a radio telescope."

"I would like materials for a . . . let us say . . . a 'mini Large Hadron Collider,'" said Heather.

"Rodney," said Joseph, "what about you?"

"For me," began Rodney, "I would like materials for the assemblage of a lunar rover so that we can get out and about on the lunar surface."

"And I would like to have some seeds of the oxygen-producing plants we have been cultivating on Mars," asked Jeremy in a somewhat demanding tone of voice.

"And I would like some stuff that I could assemble into drilling and boring equipment," said James. "Oh yes," he continued, "and ground sonar for studying subterranean geology."

"And I'm going to order spacesuits suitable for the lunar environment," said Joseph. "The ones we have with us were designed for the cold of Mars, not for the daytime heat of the moon."

CHAPTER

V

ARCHEOASTRONAUTICS ON THE MOON

F or about a month, the crew of *Mars Endeavour* came to terms with their predicament and settled down to making the best they could of their most unexpected situation on the moon. They commented upon how ironical it was that that their craft, named *Mars Endeavour*, had provided for them a lunar habitat to be their home for, what had increasingly become to be seen, an indefinite period.

Maurice Cuthbertson kept in close touch with Joseph Blackwood and his crew and ferried to the moon materials, supplies, and equipment to make their lives as bearable as possible on the harsh lunar environment. Each crew member got down to his and her own particular task. Georgina Trombers constructed her spectroscope and radio telescope, Heather Wilber soon got her mini version of the Large Hadron Collider into operation, and

Jeremy Flockston started cultivating his oxygen-producing plants in the main park of the city. James Skelton assembled his boring and drilling machines and sonar devices in one of the workshops in the city, and Joseph Blackwood and Rodney Roberts together assembled a lunar rover for long-distance travel over the lunar surface.

The lunar rover was a type of minibus, quite unlike the lunar rovers used on the later *Apollo* missions. It was capable of carrying all six members of the crew. However, it was Captain Blackwood's plan that at least two members of the crew would remain behind in *Mars Endeavour* in case of a breakdown in the "minibus." Another lunar minibus was made to operate a rescue mission if such were ever to become necessary.

The space suits that NASA sent to the crew were just like the ones the *Apollo* crews used during their lunar missions from 1969 to 1972. It was a novel experience for Joseph and his team to walk in the near-weightless environment of the moon, which has but a quarter of the Earth's gravity. *Mars Endeavour* was equipped with a device to create artificial gravity, two fast rotating magnets under the craft with their north and south poles each at opposite ends but meeting at 180 degrees of the rotation (caused by the nuclear-powered motors of the craft) created this artificial gravitation.

Harry Holbert and Margaret Woodford were twenty-two-year-old spacecraft engineers doing their internship at NASA as part of their PhD studies. They had been working at NASA for four months.

"You know," said Margaret thoughtfully to Harry one day, "considering that we were able to perform the necessary research to discover the design, materials, and methods of constructing lunar spacesuits of almost a century ago, surely we can do the same for the construction of a *Saturn V* rocket to rescue the crew of the *Mars Endeavour* from the moon."

Harry Holbert looked ceilingward and gave out a long whistle. Like his colleague Margaret, he was full of youthful energy and enthusiasm. As part of their intern responsibilities, they had been commissioned to work with Gregory Stampton, a rocket engineer working at NASA, on the rediscovery and construction of the *Apollo* mission lunar space suits and their accompanying life-support equipment. In a matter of six weeks, they had pieced together these ancient space suits and tested them successfully in artificial lunar laboratory conditions. The spacesuits were found to work perfectly well and declared to be a resounding success.

"Reconstructing spacesuits is one thing, but putting an entire lunar mission together is quite something else," responded Harry.

Harry and Margaret had made a great impression on their NASA superiors. Usually, interns were considered a nuisance by the scientists and technicians of NASA. They were supposed to be there to gain practical experience in order to give more substance to the book-learning and theory, which had been their domain of learning over the previous five years. NASA could not give away their top secret information, and the interns could not "snoop around" the premises. Generally, interns were considered as an unnecessary disruption to the serious work going on in NASA, but NASA were obliged under the terms of the grants they received from the government to take them on.

As a result of the problems created by *Mars Endeavour*, Harry and Margaret were assigned what most senior NASA personnel designated the minor task of historico-scientific research of cobbling together the *Apollo* spacesuits. No one really thought they could do it, but it kept these "pesky interns" out of mischief. It was to everyone's surprise that they actually did it. Yes, they resurrected an old piece of technology and had it fully functional.

"I think you two should have the distinction of devising a new academic discipline," said Gregory Stampton to Harry and Margaret one day. "Shall we call it 'science archaeology'?"

"In his books on Stonehenge, Sir Fred Hoyle used the term 'archeoastronomy,'" said Harry. "He firmly held that the ancient English structure of Stonehenge was an ancient astronomical observatory."

"But this is not really astronomy," replied Gregory.

"Well, what about 'archeoastronautics'?" said Margaret excitedly.

"That's it!" exclaimed Gregory. "'Archeoastronautics' fits the bill perfectly."

"Yes," agreed Harry. "I like 'archeoastronautics,' and Margaret and I are its founders." Harry then turned thoughtful and serious. "Gregory! Margaret and I have been discussing taking this, em, what we have just termed 'archeoastronautics' a bit further . . . erm mm." Harry began to stutter at this point and looked a trifle embarrassed.

"Go on," said Gregory slowly, "I'm listening."

"We have been thinking of extending our research on old spacesuits to . . . to . . . reconstructing the entire *Apollo* mission."

"I know it's a huge undertaking," said Margaret, "but we should at least consider it. I know we are only interns, but we have proved our success with the spacesuits."

Both Margaret and Harry were astonished when Gregory Stampton enthusiastically endorsed their idea. "I think that's an absolutely great idea!" he exclaimed. "Do you know something? My great-grandfather was a rocket engineer who worked on the *Apollo* missions."

"Oh! That's truly amazing," said Margaret.

"But where exactly are the plans and blueprints we need for constructing a *Saturn V* rocket and all its various parts that took the early pioneers to the moon?"

"I'll see what I can dig out of NASA's archives," said Gregory, "and I'll also see what I can find among my great-grandfather's papers in my home."

"I have been toying with a pet project of mine," said Joseph Blackwood to Rodney Roberts one day.

"What is it?" asked Rodney.

"We are in the same sea that the *Apollo 11* astronauts came down in in 1969. I was thinking of cordoning off the area in which they operated in so as to preserve it in the same condition in which Armstrong and Aldrin left it—footprints, lander, and other equipment totally undisturbed."

"It sounds a great idea," agreed Rodney. "But what exactly do you have in mind?"

"The area of operation of the *Eagle* was about the size of a football pitch. Here is a map I have retrieved from NASA intranet resources. My plan is to fence off an area the size of one and a half football pitches around the site."

"How exactly?"

"We will ask NASA for the materials and robotic equipment to construct the structure—just as we have done on Mars. If robots can perform such sophisticated feats of engineering structures on Mars, they can certainly build a fenced-off area on the moon. You and Heather Wilbur have some experience in robotics. I would rely upon you and her cooperating in programming the robots for the construction process."

An hour later, Joseph, Rodney, and Heather sat in one of *Mars Endeavour*'s restaurants discussing the project. Over dinner, they examined the details of this great undertaking.

"So is it feasible?" asked Joseph.

"We think so," said Heather.

"But it will take quite a lot of meticulous planning," said Rodney.

Arthur Watern was the director of NASA's Marshall Space Flight Center. Watern, a man in his forties, was one of those gung-ho types. He was always open to new and novel ideas. He seldom visited NASA's main center in Houston, Texas, but the circumstances surrounding the aborted mission to Mars would make these visits more frequent.

"I generally consider interns to be pests," said Arthur somewhat impatiently to Maurice Cuthbertson and Gregory Stampton. "I have a lot of important work to do and don't exactly relish the idea of having come all the way from Alabama to hear about the ideas of interns."

"You are aware," said Maurice speaking up, "that it was thanks to our two interns that the *Apollo* spacesuit technology was recovered."

"That has made it possible for the crew of the *Mars Endeavour* to walk on the surface of the moon," added Gregory. "The Martian space suits are totally inappropriate for lunar excursions."

"Yes, but recovering and constructing the entire *Apollo* space technology is quite something else," said Arthur.

"We gave Harry Holbert and Margaret Woodford the job of discovering and reconstructing the *Apollo* spacesuits just to keep them out of the way, if the honest truth be known," said Gregory. "We never seriously expected them to come up with anything. But by god, they did! They actually did!"

"These spacesuits provide one small step for the crew of *Mars Endeavour*, but a *Saturn V* rocket is a giant leap for interns." Arthur chuckled.

"Aha, not so giant as you might imagine," said Maurice in correcting tones. He then went on to explain to Arthur the project of cordoning off the *Apollo 11* landing sites. "As you know, robotic astronautics is essential for would-be scientists working for NASA and its offshoots—the Marshall Space Flight Center and the Jet

Propulsion Laboratories. It has been since way back in the 1990s and is even more so now considering that installation of habitable areas on Mars (and no doubt later on the moons of the outer gas giants) is a prerequisite for manned travel to these hostile environments."

"Could you please come to the point?" said Arthur somewhat impatiently.

"Harry and Margaret have been working with Joseph, Rodney, and Heather on the robotic programming and types of materials required for this project. They have been doing this through televisual and radio communication. Joseph, Rodney, and Heather considered Harry's and Margaret's input invaluable. They say they couldn't have done it without them."

"All right, all right!" said Arthur. "Count me in. There's no harm in trying. I suppose it's just as easy—or difficult—to rescue the crew using *Apollo* technology as it is in inventing something entirely new."

"Harry and Margaret, come in, please," said Gregory, calling out to the two interns who had been waiting in an adjoining room. They walked slowly and shyly into the presence of NASA's bigwigs. "Please explain to Dr. Watern your idea of an *Apollo* rescue mission."

"It is this," began Harry. "We provide a blueprint of the lander to Captain Blackwood and his crew. Using the robots, they reconstruct the lander with the module."

"In fact," said Margaret, "the robots construct three of them so as to carry two passengers each. Here on Earth we construct three *Saturn V* rockets. These will blast off within a week of each other and go into lunar orbit. The module from one of the landers will then dock with the orbiter and return to Earth."

"If you recover the technology, it should be feasible," agreed Arthur. "But you have overlooked something."

"What is that?" queried Harry.

"Apart from Joseph and Rodney, the other four crew members are not trained astronauts. They wouldn't know how to steer the module."

"We have, in fact, thought of that," said Harry. "Using twenty-first-century technology, the capsule containing the two crew members will be piloted by robots."

"In fact," said Margaret, "the entre mission will be controlled by astrorobots."

"It's amazing!" exclaimed Maurice.

"It's a wonderful combination and a beautiful blend of archeoastronautics and astrorobotics," said Gregory Stampton with a great big smile on his face.

"It is where the old and the new come together in a harmony of music rather than in mutual hostility and mutual exclusiveness," mused Maurice.

CHAPTER

VI

OVER THE SEA TO EAGLE

hree months after the conversation with Gregory, Maurice, Arthur, and the two interns, the robots were programmed to implement the project of preserving for posterity the site of the first moon landing. Harry and Margaret were in conversation with the *Mars Endeavour* crew by televisual communication.

"Thanks to both of you, you have made this project possible," said Joseph.

"And not only with regard to the robots," said Rodney, "but with those *Apollo* space suits."

"Tomorrow Rodney and I are going to set off south to the site where the *Eagle* landed and get cracking with the construction," said Joseph.

"Maurice Cuthbertson told us that both you young people have a plan even greater than the spacesuits and even more ambitious than the robots," said Heather Wilber.

"Yes, we do," answered Harry.

"Could you tell us about it, please?" asked Georgina.

Harry and Margaret then explained to the crew of the *Mars Endeavour* the plan they had in mind.

"I like the idea," said Jeremy Flockston.

"Yep, I'm all for it!" exclaimed James Skelton in agreement.

Joseph Blackwood instituted weekly meetings of the crew. While the general tendency had been for them to meet in twos or threes on an ad hoc basis, Joseph decided that a better degree of camaraderie could be achieved if all six came together for at least an hour each week to share the progress of their work and research. He asked them to deposit in the main computer system of *Mars Endeavour* regular updates of their own scientific endeavors.

Two months later, Joseph, acting on a suggestion from Georgina Trombers, decided to include, by means of televisual communication, Harry Holbert and Margaret Woodford in the weekly get-togethers. Despite the great achievements of Harry and Margaret in showing just how worthwhile their work had been, the "stigma" of being interns still seemed to attach to them. There was still this tendency on the part of some of the crew members to look down their noses at "mere interns." This somewhat "snobbish" attitude was soon dispelled by the amazing input of Harry and Margaret during these meetings. Recovering the old *Apollo* rocket technology was by no means an easy task, but they were getting somewhere with their researches.

"You know," said Joseph to his colleagues during the first formal meeting of the crew, "I've never really believed in meetings. During my time with NASA, I found that they only served two main purposes: bitching sessions and egoism sessions. In the former case, people whining and complaining against their colleagues or their workload; in the latter case, trying to impress their seniors by telling everyone present how brilliant their ideas were and 'well, it works for me'-type nonsense. As we are a small group, things will be different. There is no point in carping and complaining as our environment is very delicate and vulnerable in its surrounding hostile environment. And boasting about achievements is futile considering that promotional and preferment potential lies in a post-*Mars Endeavour*-cum-lunar situation. I think I am right in saying that we are all of one mind here—and that is to get off the damned moon as pronto as possible."

Heads nodded in agreement with Joseph's sentiments.

"Also," continued Joseph, "I agree with the views of Sir Fred Hoyle which consider the sciences as one seamless garment rather than as entities separated from each other in confined boxes. While the separation of biology, physics, and chemistry may be a convenient setup within the walls of academia, nature knows no such artificial distinctions."

"I fully concur with that," said Georgina Trombers in support of her leader. "I have been studying a number of galactic nebulae with the spectroscope which I constructed from the materials sent by NASA a few months ago. As there is no atmosphere here on the moon getting in the way of clear observations, I have made some amazing discoveries, namely that these nebulae are full of amino acids, and these, as we all know, are the building blocks of life. Also, the spectroscopic readings show plenty of evidence for bacteria, viruses, and even chlorophyll. I am fully convinced we live in a biological universe."

"As a bio-engineer, I can say that Georgina is right," said Jeremy Flockston in support. "I have examined the photographs and her spectrographic analyses of these gas clouds and can confirm that there is biological activity in these clouds."

"And you have something to say about the lunar rocks you have been examining, James," said Joseph.

"Using the high-powered microscopes in the labs here in the 'city,'" began James, "I saw what I thought looked like fossilized microbial material. I showed these to Jeremy, and he confirmed that that was indeed what they were."

"James and I made an even more exciting discovery," said Jeremy. "I'll let James explain it."

"Well," began James, "one of the rock samples actually had a living virus inside of it. So as not to contaminate the craft, we isolated it in a test tube."

"Was it recognizable as any terrestrial virus?" asked Joseph.

"Yes," answered Jeremy, "it was a type C virus, the one that causes respiratory symptoms in those who catch it."

"Have you discovered any bacteria in these rocks?" Heather asked James and Jeremy.

"As I say, we discovered fossilized bacterial spores," said Jeremy.

"What about living ones?"

"So far, not yet," answered James, "but Jeremy and I think it is only a matter of time before we discover viable bacteria."

"Especially after the discovery of the virus," added Jeremy.

"While there can be no doubt as to the longer-term benefits to humanity in these discoveries and in your ongoing research," said Joseph, "do any of you see any kind of practical shorter-term application in this research appertaining to the alleviation of our situation here?"

"In the long term, I see it advancing the academic discipline of astrobiology," commented Georgina. "In all honesty, I cannot see it as having any bearing upon our situation here."

"I would disagree with Georgina," came in Heather. "Jeremy, Rodney, and I have been interested in the types of bacteria that thrive on radiation. Back in 2017, Jonathon Lloyd, a geomicrobiologist at the University of Manchester in Britain, gave a presentation of his research in this area at a meeting of the Edinburgh Microbiology Society."

"Our researches showed that Lloyd and his team had thought of using these microbes as a means of disposing of nuclear waste," said Rodney. "While this proved to be successful and put paid to the arguments touted by the nuclear power dissenters, we had thought of using the properties of such bacteria as a means of locomotion."

"Also, back in 2017, there was a strain of bacteria belonging to a class termed betaproteobacteria," said Jeremy. "It was found in the soil at an old uranium ore mill in Rifle, Colorado. This type of bacteria actually breathe uranium. In a process called 'reduction,' the bacteria take a spare electron from the uranium. We had actually been considering that the energy released in this process could be used to power a spacecraft."

"Hmmm," said Joseph thoughtfully, "it would not be the most efficient way to power a craft. It is certainly better suited for its original purpose of safely disposing of nuclear waste . . ."

"But it could be sufficient to power a makeshift craft to get us off the moon and safely back to Earth," said Rodney, interrupting him.

"Just what I was about to say," said Joseph.

"So far, we haven't seen any of this bacteria in the lunar rocks," said James Skelton.

"What do you think are the chances of finding it here on the moon?" asked Heather.

"Pretty good, I would think," responded James. "Georgina has already found plenty of evidence for biological activity throughout the galaxy, and Jeremy and I have actually found a viable virus species in one of the rocks. Life can survive in the most inhospitable of places on Earth, so why can't it do the same throughout the universe? The moon, having no protective atmosphere and little to nothing of a magnetic field, it is constantly being bombarded by cosmic rays from outer space and solar rays from the sun."

"Considering that certain bacteria can not only survive but actually thrive on nuclear waste, there is no reason to doubt that the same type of bacteria can survive the radiation of outer space and thrive on the nuclear products of gas clouds created by supernova explosions," said Georgina.

"Heather, you want to say something about this?"

"Yes," answered Heather. "I had been thinking of introducing into my mini LHC something that has never been tried before in this kind of equipment. It is biological material. I would like to work closely with Georgina regarding how life, at its most basic forms—viruses and bacteria, might possibly be produced in stellar explosions. My idea is to simulate such an explosion in the mini LHC and introduce the betaproteobacteria's DNA to artificially create betaproteobacteria. You and Rodney can then work out some way of using the radioactivity from moon rock to power a spacecraft."

"Rodney and I will work on the engine and design of such a craft once we know more about the bacteria and its properties and processes," said Joseph.

"What about the efforts of NASA's two interns?" asked Georgina.

"They should continue with their archeoastronautical efforts," said Joseph, "as there is, as things stand, a better chance of them successfully reconstructing a *Saturn V* than we of constructing a bacteria-powered nuclear spacecraft."

"Well, here is a comprehensive design of the old *Saturn V* rocket," said Gregory Stampton to Harry Holbert and Margaret Woodford one day.

"That gives us a lot to go on," said Harry. "When Margaret and I have worked out the intricacies of its engines, we need to obtain the materials for its construction."

"It was built mainly of aluminum," said Gregory. "You two look over the details and try to figure out how you are going to put it all together."

"May I ask where you found this information from?" queried Margaret.

"As I said before, my great-grandfather worked on the original *Apollo* missions. He was meticulous about keeping records."

"Why did he keep them in his own personal files?" continued Margaret with her questioning. "Sorry for sounding rather interrogative, but it suggests to me that your great-grandfather was an insightful man who anticipated the loss of this technology."

"You are very clever," answered Gregory. "In 1972, when my great-grandfather saw that the *Apollo* project was coming to an end and that due mainly to budgetary restraints, we would not be returning to the moon for quite some time, he realized that NASA would somewhat carelessly abandon the entire corpus of *Apollo* technology. He had already seen how slipshod NASA was at preserving its files and technological achievements, so he decided to take matters into his own hands."

"So he made the crucial decision to save this vast array of technology?" said Harry.

"Exactly!" said Gregory. "NASA wanted to classify the *Apollo* technology as 'dead files'—in other words, lose it, as my great-grandfather always said. However, Robert James Stampton never believed in the concept of 'dead files.' He preferred to call them 'dormant files.' He would often say that you never know when a file may have to be resurrected to meet an entirely unthought-of contingency."

"Wow!" exclaimed Harry. "It's almost as if your great-grandfather prophesied the disaster with the *Mars Endeavour*."

"Yes, indeed—yes, indeed," said Gregory, nodding in contemplative agreement.

"Do you think his files contain everything needed to put Humpty Dumpty together again?" said Margaret half jestingly.

"My great-grandfather was highly methodical and extremely meticulous," said Gregory reassuringly. "However, I will also look in NASA's files so that we can do comparative analyses with what we have here. NASA's files are nowhere near as comprehensive as my great-grandfather's, but they should be worthwhile drawing on."

"Let's get started as soon as possible—like right now," said Harry somewhat impatiently.

Harry and Margaret started with the basic structure of the massive *Saturn V* rocket itself. They studied its intricacies of design and decided that they would soon be able to look at the detailed engineering of its component parts. Gregory Stampton made available to them a host of material for their perusal. With their knowledge of rocketry, the two interns grew increasingly confident about how they would proceed with the rocket's reconstruction. Day by day, they saw in their young minds the coming together of old technology. It astonished them to think that old technology would come to the rescue of the crew of a state-of-the-art spaceship which originally had been destined for Mars and had, for unknown reasons, come to find itself on the moon.

Joseph Blackwood and Rodney Roberts had taken sufficient oxygen and food supplies for a two-week journey to the site where the *Apollo 11* astronauts made history by being the first men to walk on the moon. The powerful atomic motors of the minibus were able to haul seven trailers full of robots and materials for the project of cordoning off the site.

After a five-day journey, the lunar bus reached the area of the *Apollo 11* landing site. Joseph stopped the convoy of bus and trailers well outside of the area in which Armstrong and Aldrin had operated in. He did not want to disturb as much as one footprint in the area. As the moon has no atmosphere, objects appear to be closer than they actually are. The fact that the curvature of the moon is more pronounced than that of the Earth's because of the moon's being only a quarter of the Earth's size also contributes to this distance-reducing illusion.

Gazing through the windows of the bus, the two astronauts were in awe of what they saw. There was the lunar lander. There was the rectangular piece of equipment for measuring the solar wind. There was the American flag, standing proudly erect in the bleak lunar surface. There was the ladder from which Neil Armstrong descended and pronounced the eternal words, no doubt still fleeting their way across the galaxy and out to the far-flung clusters of galaxies strewn throughout this vast universe, to be picked up by other civilizations on habitable planets orbiting a myriad of suns warming and nourishing the great mystery which we call life, life of which we are all a part of in a supra-galactic ocean of humanity, "that's one small step for a man, one giant leap for mankind." The atmosphere-devoid moon, whose sky no desert on Earth could render an air-clear parallel and whose stars no fuller on Earth could whiten to cause them to shine with such fiery brilliance, minded Joseph to understand Armstrong's words in a way no man had hitherto understood them, for Joseph could not help but think of Armstrong's "mankind" as being the mankind that extends itself throughout the eternal universe, life hosted by an endless array of worlds throbbing with the passion of mankind.

After this reverie, Joseph and Rodney offloaded two "master robots" from the trailer. They were programmed to "supervise" the work of the other robots and robotic-type equipment which would build a protective dome around the perimeter of the site. The forty-foot-high dome was made of a new type of material called reinforced concrete plastic. It was so strong that even an army tank moving at one hundred miles per hour could not penetrate, yet it was as crystal clear as to give the impression that nothing was there. Future astronauts and space tourists could look at the sight but would be unable to hive off souvenirs from the artifacts left by Armstrong and Aldrin. Cameras with telescopic lenses would enable visitors to view the site at close range, yet not as much as one of Armstrong's or Aldrin's footprints would be obliterated.

It took the robotic equipment only three days to complete the task. Joseph and Rodney proudly surveyed their work.

"Well," said Joseph, "that is the *Apollo 11* lunar landing site preserved for posterity."

"Yes," agreed Rodney. "Now that we see what a success this has been, let's think about doing the same for the other five lunar landing sites."

"That will be our next project," said Joseph. "Come on, let's get these robots and the equipment back on to the trailers and head back to *Mars Endeavour.*"

CHAPTER

VII

DAMNED POLITICS AND POLITICIANS

S en. Vincent Tucker headed the newly-formed Science and Technology Committee. It was composed of six members of the House of Representative and six members of the Senate. Their brief was to control public spending in the areas of scientific research and to decide where taxpayers' money should be allocated in terms of which organization should be awarded grants and how much they were to be given.

It had come to the attention of the STC that 70 percent of the budget for science and technology was given to NASA. Various scientific research organizations protested what they saw as a disproportionate allocation of money for space research. NASA countered with the argument that space projects embraced all scientific disciplines. They cited advances in astrobiology, which pointed toward a greater degree of biological activity in the universe. Analyses of interstellar gas clouds showed highly sophisticated chemistry taking place. Spectroscopic analyses of interstellar dust indicated the presence of desiccated bacteria and that that bacteria was carried to planets via comets. So here were connections between astronomy, space projects, biology, chemistry, and medicine. Therefore, when Maurice Cuthbertson was arguing his case for the continuation of the same levels of funding for NASA, he told the committee that the 70 percent was a case of "lies, damned lies, and statistics," as the benefits of this expenditure percolated down to all branches of science. Unfortunately, Sen. Vincent Tucker and the other twelve members of the STC did not see it Cuthbertson's way. NASA's allocation was to be immediately slashed to 40 percent of STC budgetary allocations.

A day after the STC hearings, Maurice called an emergency meeting with Arthur Watern, director of the Marshall Space Flight Center, and Gregory Stampton, NASA's head of rocket technology. He sat down in his chair behind his desk in his office. The mood was serious and somber.

"I think you are both aware of the serious consequences of this massive budgetary cutback," began Maurice.

"Yes," responded Arthur. "It means we will have to make massive reductions on our Mars projects."

"Upgrading of our current atomic-powered spacecraft will have to be put on hold," said Gregory gloomily.

"Flights to Mars and beyond will have to wait a long time," groaned Arthur.

"Bad as that is," came in Maurice, "there is worse to come."

"What is it?" asked Gregory.

"I have had intense discussions with Senator Tucker and his two confidants in the STC," said Maurice. "It's concerning the crew of *Mars Endeavour*."

"And?" responded Arthur is somewhat quizzical tones.

"And," said Maurice with an exasperated sigh, "I'd rather you hear this straight from the horse's mouth. Tucker will come here tomorrow, and he, you two, me, and the two interns will have a meeting, by televisual, with Joseph Blackwood and his crew."

The following day Maurice called his staff together and Jeremy called his. The televisual conference was set up and all were keen to hear what Sen. Vincent Tucker had to say. They anticipated that whatever it may be, the news would be bad.

"Administrator Maurice Cuthbertson, Captain Joseph Blackwood," began Tucker, "as you know, due to the economic downturn in the US economy, it has behooved the government to make cutbacks in all areas of expenditure. NASA, like every other sector which depends on government largesse, has to take its fair share of the cutbacks. While it is the government's and NASA's top priority to rescue you from the moon, there are simply insufficient funds to develop a craft which can safely take you off the moon."

There were gasps of shock both on the Earth and moon at this. Joseph and his team looked at one another in a state of stunned stupor. Maurice and his staff gazed in horrified amazement at what Tucker had just said.

"What do you mean?" said Joseph. "Are you going to leave us on the moon to die?"

"No," replied Tucker. "It's not quite like that."

"Could you elaborate on this a bit more, please, Senator?" requested Maurice.

"You have supplies for at least three years. That was the original plan for the Mars project. We expect you to use these supplies in conjunction with what you can grow in the farming areas of *Mars Endeavour*. On top of this, we will continue to ferry supplies to you by unmanned spacecraft."

"Are you saying that Captain Blackwood and his crew are to be permanent residents of the moon?" asked Arthur Watern.

"No," replied Tucker. "When the economy improves and budgetary allocations are increased, work on the development of a lunar rescue mission can proceed. But it may be a few years away."

"Is there any way that you can persuade the powers-that-be," asked Rodney Roberts, "to upgrade the priority levels for our rescue from the moon?"

"I can only promise to do my very best in this regard," replied the senator.

After another half hour of questions and answers, Senator Tucker once again gave his apologies and took leave of the meeting.

"I can only suggest," said Maurice, "that all of you there on the moon carry on your projects as best you can. We'll do the best we can with the fewer resources we have at our disposal."

"What about our project to piece together the *Saturn V*?" asked Harry Holbert anxiously.

"We'll have to look into the costs of that operation, Harry," replied Maurice.

"But wouldn't it be cheaper than having to plan and develop the entire new type of rescue craft?" asked Margaret Woodford.

"I'm not sure yet, Margaret," replied Maurice rather sadly. "I'll have to sit down with NASA's accountants and engineers and work out a cost analysis of it all."

"Damn it all," said Joseph to his crew at one of their meetings. "If they can't build a rescue craft on Earth, then we'll jolly well build one here on the moon."

"I've just had a communique directly from Vincent Tucker," said James Skelton.

"That's rather unusual," said Joseph. "Any such communique should come directly to me as captain. I don't mean to sound egotistical, but this is a strange deviation from protocol. Well, in fact, it should have gone first to Maurice, then to me, and then on to you."

"I also am somewhat mystified," said James.

"Is it anything of a classified nature, or can in be read out to us all, James?" asked Joseph.

"In fact, it is a rather mundane request."

"Please enlighten us, James."

"It simply asks me to carry out a geological survey of the region of within a twenty-mile radius of the city and to take core samples at as many and varied locations as possible."

"It is indeed a rather mundane request," agreed the captain, "but it is a very strange one considering that our main priority is to keep ourselves alive until rescue is made possible."

"If we have these orders," said James, "we had better follow them. Perhaps the more we cooperate with them, the greater the chance of their prioritizing our rescue."

"From my great-grandfather's papers," said Gregory Stampton to Harry and Margaret, "I can locate where exactly we can find the actual component parts of the *Saturn V* rocket. Here is the list."

SATURN 1
US Space & Rocket Center, Huntsville, AL

SATURN 1B
Kennedy Space Center, FL

SATURN V
Kennedy Space Center, FL

SATURN V
US Space & Rocket Center, Huntsville, AL

SATURN V
Johnson Space Center, NASA, Houston, TX

F-1 ENGINES
National Air and Space Museum, Washington, DC
US Space and Rocket Center, Huntsville, AL
NASA Johnson Space Center, Houston, TX
Kalamazoo Aviation History Museum (Air Zoo), Kalamazoo, MI
New Mexico Museum of Space History, Alamogordo, NM

Powerhouse Museum, Sydney, Australia

NASA Marshall Space Flight Center, Huntsville, AL

"Ah! That's magic!" exclaimed Harry. "With actual physical parts and the diagrams, we can all the sooner put together the entire rocket."

"Yes, we can," said Margaret excitedly.

James Skelton spent an entire week surveying the area the STC asked him to survey. He took numerous core samples and sonar soundings. He carried the core samples back to his lab in *Mars Endeavour* and subjected them to analyses. He then looked at the sonar sounding graphs and compared these with the samples. What he saw absolutely astonished him. He went straight to Joseph Blackwood.

"That is just astounding, James, just astounding. The area is no less than a massive gold mine," said Joseph.

James became very thoughtful and pensive. Both he and Joseph were silent for a few minutes. At last, Joseph spoke up.

"I smell a rat in all this!" exclaimed Joseph.

"Great minds think alike," responded James.

"Are you thinking what I'm thinking?"

"You mean that the engine failure on *Mars Endeavour* was no freak accident at all?"

"Snap!" blurted out Joseph.

"It seems we have been sent here to mine the area robotically and supervise the sending of the ore back to Earth."

"Yes!" said Joseph angrily. Joseph again became very thoughtful. At last, he said, "I have a strategy to deal with this. First of all, do not tell the rest of the crew about the deposits of gold. And then . . ." Joseph, in an air of great hush and secrecy, went on to explain to James his strategy. "And now," he said, "I'm going to make another examination of the *Mars Endeavour*'s engines—a more thorough one than I made the last time."

"At last, we have a detailed design of the lunar lander module," said Margaret.

"Yes!" said Harry excitedly. "Gregory's great-grandfather did an amazing job of technology preservation."

"You guys really are superb archaeoastronautics!" said Gregory. "Now here's a map of where we can find the command and service modules so we can make our research more three-dimensional."

"I've been wondering about the government cutbacks and how they will affect this project," said Harry.

"Maurice will decide how the budget is allocated within NASA. He is on our side, so I think everything will be all right," said Gregory in reassuring tones to Harry's concerns.

"So we can proceed according to plan?" inquired Margaret.

"Yes, indeed," said Gregory.

"Well, James," said Joseph. "I've made a minute examination of *Mars Endeavour*'s engines."

"And?" responded James, all ears.

"There is nothing the matter with the engines. They are in pristine condition."

"So how is the malfunction to be explained?"

Joseph laid a small metal container on the desk. He opened it and took out twenty-five little devices, each about the size of a pinky nail.

"What are these?" asked James.

"Laboratory examination of these tiny digital devices reveal them to be means by which the craft's engines can be controlled from Earth."

James gaped in awe and shock, his jaw almost hitting the floor. For about a minute, he stood there speechless.

"Should we tell the crew?" James asked, eventually finding his voice.

"The fewer people who know about this, the better," answered Joseph, "at least at this stage."

Eventually, Vincent Tucker got on the televisual communicative system for a live conference with Joseph and James.

"So have you completed the geological survey of the area, Dr. Skelton, as the STC requested of you?"

"Yes," replied James.

"And could you explain to me and my fellow committee members the results of your survey?"

"Like most of the lunar mare, and the Mare Tranquillitatis being no exception, my geological survey found the area to be composed mainly of a variety of basaltic compounds, thus indicating volcanic eruptions at various periods in the moon's geological history."

"What about other substances?" continued Tucker in somewhat pressing tones.

"Apart from a few trace metals, mainly of iron, the area is simple volcanic basalt."

"Did you take core samples—I mean, from below the surface?"

"Yes."

"And did these yield anything other than basaltic compounds?" asked Tucker, becoming increasingly impatient.

"No," responded James quite simply.

"What about sonar soundings?" The senator was by now beginning to show signs of exasperation.

"The same basaltic materials are detectable to a depth of three thousand feet."

"I don't think you have made a thorough enough examination of the area, Dr. Skelton," blurted out Tucker in rather lofty tones.

"Are you a qualified geologist and miner, Senator Tucker? I am. Furthermore, I am on the moon, and you are not."

It was clear now that the exchanges between James and Tucker were becoming heated. It was clear to both Joseph and James that Tucker expected a confirmation of the gold veins under the surface of this area of the Mare Tranquillitatis.

"You have performed this survey," went on Tucker, "and all you can give me is basaltic material."

"Senator Tucker," replied James, his tone of voice rising to an increasingly angrier pitch, "I am merely reporting the results of my survey findings. I did not make this mare. If you are not satisfied with its geological composition, I suggest you take the issue up with the Almighty, but please, kindly, do not question my integrity and professionalism as a geologist."

"Captain Blackwood," said Tucker, addressing Joseph directly, "may I suggest you restrain this member of your crew somewhat?"

"Senator Tucker," responded Joseph in a calm and relaxed manner, "Dr. Skelton is merely giving you the facts of his findings. Look, I don't mean to sound facetious, Senator, but did you expect him to come up with silver and gold?"

With that, Tucker huffily and abruptly disconnected the televisual conference and ended the meeting.

CHAPTER
VIII
POLITICS AND SPACE

"**W**ell, kids," said Gregory Stampton to Harry and Margaret one morning, "I've got some pretty bad news for you."

"What is it?" asked Harry.

"The STC is cutting off funding for the reconstruction of the *Apollo* program," replied Gregory nervously, not knowing what reaction he would get from the two interns.

Harry stood there shocked; Margaret was almost in tears.

"But didn't NASA's cost accountants work out that rebuilding the old *Apollo* program would be cheaper than developing an entirely new kind of craft?" said Margaret.

"Yes, but Senator Tucker and his STC buddies have different ideas for budgetary allocations," said Gregory with a sigh.

"Rodney," said Joseph to his rocket engineer one day, "do you know how I could set up a televisual conference with Maurice without anyone else being able to pick up the signals?"

"You mean you don't want Tucker and his team in on certain areas of our communication with Earth?" queried Rodney.

"Exactly," responded Joseph.

Rodney became thoughtful for a moment. Eventually, he spoke up. "I think I can do it via a lunar antenna directly linked to Maurice's office."

"How long will it take you, do you think, to set up this antenna?"

"Not too long. Give me a couple of days."

Harry and Margaret sat looking extremely despondent in their workshop when Gregory walked in.

"Why the long faces?" asked Gregory.

"I think you know," responded Margaret drearily.

"Well, this time, I have some more cheering news for you."

"Which is?" asked Harry.

"I've been talking to a private space commercial company," said Gregory. "It is called New Space Horizons. They have agreed to provide the financing for the *Apollo* program on condition that NASA can fund at least 20 percent of the operation."

"That's the sticking point," said Harry.

"Tucker isn't going to agree to it," said Margaret.

"I know, I know," said Gregory, changing his mood from optimism to pessimism.

"Well, Joseph, the antenna is set up. You should have privacy in your conversations with NASA or whoever you want to contact back on Earth," said Rodney.

"Thanks, Rodney, I appreciate your efforts," responded Joseph with genuine gratitude.

Rodney left Joseph's office. Joseph then called James in.

"Rodney's done a great job in setting up the antenna," Joseph told James. "I now intend to call Maurice straight away."

During the televisual session, Joseph and James explained the situation to Maurice and Gregory.

"Do you think the two interns should be apprised of this?" asked Joseph.

"They are young, but they are intelligent and mature," responded Gregory.

"I think they can be trusted to keep a secret," said Maurice.

Gregory called in Harry and Margaret to take part in the televisual conference. Joseph briefed them on what they had discovered on the Mare Tranquillitatis.

"It comes as no surprise to us," said Harry. "In fact, Margaret and I have been doing some Internet research on Vincent Tucker."

"And?" said Joseph, listening intently.

"He is a consultant to a company called Ore Mining Enterprises," said Margaret. "The company specializes in mining precious metals."

"What intrigues me," said James, "is as to how Tucker and his associates knew about the gold in this section of the mare."

"We discovered," explained Harry, "that Ore Mining Enterprises, commissioned a private space commercial company named Planet Outreach, to send a satellite to perform a geological survey of the moon. Using state-of-the art technology, its sonar could penetrate well below the surface of the moon. They discovered a few veins of gold and silver on both sides of the moon but not in commercial quantities but with this one exception."

"My own ground survey," said James, "shows that the veins in this part of the mare would yield vast profits."

"But this company surely is involved in terrestrial mining," said Maurice. "Why this sudden interest in lunar ore extraction?"

"We discovered," said Margaret, "that OME's gold mine in California is near exhaustion levels. In order to survive, the company needs new gold fields. Practically all these are already being mined by other companies."

"But that satellite must have cost OME a pretty penny," said Gregory. "How are they going to pay PO for this?"

"OME and PO have made an agreement that they will split the profits from a mining operation 50/50. So it's a win-win situation for both," explained Margaret.

"The satellite which made the survey was then instructed to crash on the far side of the moon," said Harry.

"So basically, Tucker wants to keep us here to perform his mining operations," said James.

"Yes, it seems so," said Harry. "His plan is for OME and PO to send you guys on *Mars Endeavour*, robotic mining equipment. He will then send craft to the moon to collect the ore and return it to Earth."

Maurice looked extremely puzzled and asked Harry and Margaret how they knew all this.

"It's not exactly the kind of thing that would be splashed on the Internet and grid for all and sundry to see," said Maurice. "How can you possibly verify all this?"

Harry looked thoughtful for a moment. He took a deep breath and said, "My uncle, Rupert Holbert, is a space mechanical engineer with PO. He recently resigned because of the highly unethical way the company had manipulated *Mars Endeavour* to make an emergency landing on the moon. He told me everything. However, I must ask you, for the safety of my uncle, not to divulge this information far and wide."

"Did your uncle give you permission to divulge the information to us?" asked Gregory.

"Yes, he did. He is a Christian man of the highest principles and ethics and wishes to cooperate with NASA fully in rescuing the crew of the *Mars Endeavour*. But he will do this behind the scenes for the sake of his own protection."

"Now what I'd like to know," said James, "is how these tiny robotic devices were attached to the engines of *Mars Endeavour*."

Harry looked sad and downcast. "My Uncle Rupert attached them. As you know, the engines of *Mars Endeavour* were designed in a cooperative venture between NASA and PO. Although my uncle knew they were guidance systems for the craft, he did not know the sinister purposes for which they were intended."

"At what stage in the game did your uncle twig to the bad intentions of Tucker, PO, and OME?" asked Maurice.

"First of all, he was extremely puzzled as to how a craft of such advanced and intricate design could have malfunctioned so soon after its takeoff. When he heard about the satellite sent to make a geological survey of the moon and the discovery of commercial quantities of gold in the very part of the Mare Tranquillitatis, where the *Mars Endeavour* came down, and then the cutbacks to NASA projects, the postponement of the *Apollo* project, he started to put two and two together."

"Did your uncle make known to PO the reasons for his resignation?" asked James.

"For his own safety, he had to give a reason other than the real one to account for his decision to leave the company?"

"Which was?" asked Joseph.

"That he wished to work directly with NASA on interplanetary craft projects."

"I think, for your uncle's safety as well as for his integrity, I think we should hire him," said Maurice.

"But will Tucker not suspect something anyway, considering that we simply do not have the budget for the development of interplanetary craft?" said Gregory.

"He will be hired simply for their design but not for their construction," said Maurice.

"Sorry for all the questions, Harry," said Joseph, "but who designed the tiny robotic guidance systems for the engines, and who controlled them?"

"It was a collaborative effort between my uncle and a team of engineers. They were merely meant to be backup guidance systems for the engines. Before they were placed on the engines of the *Mars Endeavour*, they must have been adjusted to perform their evil function."

"No one informed us of these 'robotic guidance devices,'" said Maurice.

"Of course not," said Harry, "they were surreptitiously placed there by the engineer, or engineers, during the fitting process."

"So what happens next?" asked Joseph. "What should our strategy be?"

"Carry on with your projects there," advised Maurice. "Here on Earth, we'll see what we can do regarding the archeoastronautics project and try to rebuild the *Saturn V* rocket. However, in the more immediate term, we'll have to see what Tucker's next move is going to be."

"Harry! Margaret!" said Gregory. "Come and meet Dr. Daniel North, the president of New Space Horizons."

Harry and Margaret greeted Dr. North enthusiastically.

"Gregory has fully briefed me on the situation regarding *Mars Endeavour*," said North, "and how it relates to Senator Tucker, the PO, OME, and your uncle, Harry . . . I have a plan regarding how to solve this issue," said North.

"We would be most interested in hearing about it, Dr. North," said Margaret.

"I want to explain it to you and to Joseph and James. Let's set up the televisual communications."

Daniel outlined his plans to all concerned and cautioned all to keep the utmost secrecy.

"Why don't you see more than just basaltic material?" asked Tucker of Joseph and James during a televisual conference.

"Because that is all we can find, Senator Tucker," answered James.

"Look," said Tucker, softening his approach a bit, "let me come perfectly clean with you."

"Oh! Please do that, Senator," replied Joseph in rather sneering tones.

"Five months ago, we sent a satellite to make a geological survey of the moon, and we discovered a large deposit of gold in the northern part of the Mare Tranquillitatis. And we want you to mine the ore and return it to Earth. We will then have the financial wherewithal to develop the means to bring you guys back to Earth."

"And it just so happened, Senator," said James, "that our craft came down exactly in the area of mining operations?"

Tucker, gulping and clearing his throat, simply said, "Well, eh, yes . . . yes!"

"Senator Tucker," said Joseph, "do you think we were born yesterday? Do you take us for fools?"

"Look!" said Tucker, going red in the face, "if you and your crew wish to get off the moon, I suggest you cooperate with the mining operation." And with that, he ended the televisual.

"You know," said Daniel, who had just watched a recording of the televisual communication, "Tucker and his lot can never let Joseph and his crew off the moon."

"Why not?" asked Harry.

"Because," explained Daniel, "first of all, he needs humans there to supervise the robots in their mining operations. Robotic mining technology has not yet developed to the stage whereby robots can perform the mining operations without human control. And secondly, if they returned to Earth, they would inform the legal authorities about all of this and have Tucker et al arrested."

"Anyway, we have our plan," said Maurice, "just keep it hush."

CHAPTER
IX
MINING ON THE MOON

O ver the next three months, supply craft with robotic mining equipment from Planet Outreach arrived on the moon. These were installed by Joseph, James, and Rodney. At the same time, robotic mining equipment from New Space Horizons also reached the *Mars Endeavour* crew. These were likewise duly set up to conduct their mining operations too. However, the mining operations of the PO equipment and the NSH equipment were set up ten miles apart. Fifty tons of mined material were loaded on to the cargo craft sent by PO and fifty tons on to the craft sent by NSH. Both set off from the moon on their four-day journey to Earth. Tucker was informed of this consignment, and through the special antenna, Maurice, Gregory, Daniel, and the two interns were informed of theirs.

On the televisual, Daniel congratulated Joseph and James on performing such a fine job.

"We are financially well on the way to getting your *Saturn V* rocket built," said Daniel to Gregory, Harry, and Margaret.

"You wanted all this kept secret from the rest of the crew, Joseph. How have you been able to do this?"

"I realized that preserving the *Apollo 11* landing site would now be more than just a pet hobby of mine," said Joseph. "I've sent the rest of the crew to the other sites with robotic equipment to do exactly the same. In due course, we'll tell them what it's all about. They should return in about a month."

Tucker and the top executives of OME and PO were in the launch and landing area of PO. The consignment of lunar material had just arrived. On close inspection of the material, Tucker and his partners in crime went ballistic. They were greeted with a deluge of dust, gravel, and pieces of rock when they opened the containers.

"What the blazes is that you sent, Blackwood? What do you think you're playing at?"

"Listen to me, Tucker," responded Joseph, "you insisted that there was gold in this area. We informed you that there was not. Perhaps you will believe us now. It is our burning priority to get off the moon, so if there had been gold, we would have sent it to you."

"But our geological surveyor satellite clearly indicated gold ore reserves in that area in which you landed."

"Well," said James, "perhaps either your satellite was wrong or you misinterpreted the readings from the sonar soundings. Look, Senator, can you display the sonar readings for me now?"

With the help of the PO technical personnel, the readings were shown to James. "These parts of the soundings, which you have mistakenly thought of as being gold, in fact, show pyrite—or more commonly called fool's gold."

"But our geologists said it was real gold," protested Tucker.

"Oh, well then," responded James, "you'd better get new geologists."

"You listen to me, Blackwood, you and your crew had better settle down for a long, long stay on the moon—perhaps even a permanent one!"

Rupert Holbert was a man in his early fifties. Although a brilliant space engineer, he was quiet and unassuming in his demeanor.

"I'm afraid that under current financial stringencies, we cannot pay you as much as PO did," said Maurice honestly.

"That's quite all right," responded Rupert understandingly. "The main concern is not pay but rescuing our friends on the moon."

"Thank you for your understanding," said Maurice.

"My nephew and his friend Margaret are going to reconstruct a *Saturn V* rocket. How are we going to explain the construction to Tucker and his colleagues?"

"Indeed," said Maurice, "we can't hide something of such gigantic proportions."

"Even the massive hangar in which it will be built won't be enough as there will be hundreds of engineers and technicians working on its construction."

Three days later, Maurice and Rupert brought the issue of secrecy before Daniel North.

"The reason is this," suggested Daniel, "that because of financial constraints, we have had to resort to old technology for sending satellites into lower Earth orbit."

"Well done, all of you!" said Joseph to his crew. "You've done a great job in preserving the *Apollo* landing sites."

"Thanks," said Heather. "It means a lot to us too. It's part of our nation's heritage."

"May I ask about how things are progressing with the rescue mission?" said Georgina.

"And have these mining operations anything to do with it?" asked Rodney.

Giving his crew part of the story, Joseph informed them of how James had found gold in commercial quantities and that NSH would use the proceeds from the sale of the gold to help in the construction a *Saturn V* rocket. This greatly boosted the morale of the crew.

With hard work and perseverance, the *Saturn V* rocket was ready. Maurice, Gregory, Harry, Margaret, and Daniel informed the crew of *Mars Endeavour* that they should select two of their number to sit in the capsule part of the lander when it touched down on the surface of the moon. The capsule would then dock with the command module which would convey the selected members back to Earth.

The capsule will take off leaving the lander section on the moon and will dock with the command module.

As Georgina and Heather were the two female crew members, Joseph insisted that they should go first. As captain, Joseph would be among the last two to leave. Three days were spent in which Harry and Margaret instructed Heather and Georgina and the rest of the crew how to proceed once the lunar lander reached the moon's surface. This was done using simulation training through televisual link.

Confident that the crew were ready, the massive *Saturn V* rocket lifted off from Cape Canaveral and was on its way to the moon. Joseph and his crew were informed that the lunar module would separate from the command module and land on the moon in five days. The selected landing site was a relatively smooth plain-like area about three miles from *Mars Endeavour*.

A couple of days after the launch, Rupert, with his nephew Harry, and with Margaret, Gregory and Daniel, came into Maurice's office with a panic-stricken look on his face.

"What on Earth is the matter?" asked Maurice concernedly. He was surprised as Rupert was, by nature, a calm and collected man. Rupert proceeded to explain a very alarming situation that had just developed and necessitated getting the rest of the crew off the moon as soon as possible.

"How do you know all this, Rupert?" asked Maurice.

"I have an insider mole in PO. He and I are of the same ethical ilk. He told me that he would stay on with PO so that he could inform me of any sinister goings-on that I would need to be aware of."

"Can we muster the finances to build two *Saturn V* rockets at the same time? And this time, hopefully, we can complete them in four months?" Rupert asked.

"By working round the clock and hiring another fifty skilled personnel, I reckon it could be done. I think another shipment of fifty tons of gold ore would provide the necessary finance for the rockets," said Maurice.

"And in order not to panic the crew," said Gregory, "I think we should not inform them of Tucker's wicked plan."

"We feel so guilty at leaving you here," said Georgina to her friends.

"We feel like we are abandoning our friends and posts," added Heather.

"Don't think like that," said Rodney. "We'll be following you all very soon."

"Come on, you two," said Joseph, "get into your lunar suits, and I'll drive you to the lander."

As they drove up to the lunar lander, Joseph, Georgina, and Heather were awestruck.

"You know," said Joseph, "it's like the rerun of an old film. I'm almost expecting to see Neil Armstrong come out of the module and say once more those immortal words, 'that's one small step for man, one giant leap for mankind.'"

Joseph then made sure that Georgina and Heather were safely ensconced in the capsule and that the hatch was firmly closed. He then drove back to *Mars Endeavour*, and using the antenna that Rodney had set up, he sent the message to Maurice and his team in NASA—"all ready for liftoff."

The four remaining crew members watched the ascent of the capsule. Up, up, and away it went, carrying Heather and Georgina. Half an hour later, the module, by robotic remote control from Earth, successfully docked with the command module. Heather and Georgina climbed out of the capsule and into the command module.

Once they were inside, the command service module jettisoned the ascent stage of the lunar module that had carried Georgina and Heather from the moon. The CSM then began its five-day journey back home. And it was all controlled from Earth.

Five days later, the remaining part of the spacecraft, the conical nose of the command module, parachuted down on to the landing site of Cape Canaveral. Georgina and Heather emerged from the interior. They seemed to be in quite good health after being cooped up for so long in such a confined space.

After a day's rest, they were debriefed by Maurice and introduced to Harry and Margaret.

"You two are more than amazing," said Heather. "If it hadn't been for you two, we'd still be on the moon."

"We can't thank you enough," said Georgina, trying to hold back the tears and giving Harry and Margaret huge hugs of gratitude.

Maurice and his inner circle (Gregory, Daniel, Harry, Rupert, and Margaret) informed Georgina and Heather of Tucker's desire to keep them on the moon so that he and his accomplices at PO and OME could make profits from the gold deposits on the mare. They did not, however, tell the two ladies of Tucker's more wicked plan.

"I know you two ladies would like to get in touch with your families as soon as possible, but until we get everyone from *Mars Endeavour* off the moon, we must keep your return top secret," said Maurice.

"Secrecy for the moment is key to the successful operation of rescuing your friends from the moon," added Gregory.

"We would kindly ask you two ladies to stay here in NASA accommodation until mission accomplished."

Both Heather and Georgina, understanding the sensitive nature of the crisis, agreed to do just that.

Two weeks later, another consignment of ore arrived from the moon. This time it was not fifty but seventy tons of the precious metal.

"We have more than enough now to build the two *Saturn V* rockets needed for Operation Lunar Rescue," said Joseph to his team.

CHAPTER

X

A RACE AGAINST THE CLOCK

F our months later and the next *Saturn V* rocket was wheeled onto the launching pad at Cape Canaveral. Three days later, after a thorough check, it was ready to fly to the moon. Just after blast off, Maurice Cuthbertson had an unexpected visitor.

"Dr. Cuthbertson, I am here in the official capacity of the chairman of the Science and Technology Committee, the all-House committee, on the allocation of grants to science research bodies," said Vincent Tucker in pompous and lofty tones. Although Tucker knew that Maurice Cuthbertson knew his position and the purpose of the committee he headed, his mentioning of it was by way of threat. It was as if to say "I can cut off your funding at the drop of a hat."

"And how can I be of assistance to you, Senator Tucker?" responded Maurice in a calm and subdued manner.

"It has come to the attention of my committee that a *Saturn V* rocket was launched from here four months ago. I also hear that two more are under construction."

"You have heard right, Senator."

"I thought I gave orders for the cessation of the archeoastronautics project until further notice."

"Mr. Tucker! Due to the worse-than-expected severity of the budgetary restraints imposed upon us by your committee, we have had to resort to using the old technology to ferry supplies to the crew of the *Mars Endeavour*. In order to eke out our budget, we have entered into a partnership project with New Space Horizons, a company that specializes in satellite technology and in developing interplanetary space vehicles."

"A company that is developing interplanetary space vehicles is coming to you for archaic technology? I'm not a scientist, Dr. Cuthbertson, but I am not altogether technologically illiterate."

"I am not an economist, Senator, but I know that NSH, like other private commercial space vehicle manufacturers, is also feeling the pinch due to the cutbacks. Your budgetary restraints have had a percolating effect, Senator."

"I want to speak to all the crew members, all six of them right this instant," demanded Tucker.

Maurice had to do some quick thinking at this sudden demand from Tucker.

"Well, em," began Maurice, "ehm, that would not be possible at the moment."

"And uh, pray tell me, why not?" said Tucker with a victorious-looking grin on his face.

"Because only Capt. Joseph Blackwood and James Skelton are at the main *Mars Endeavour* base."

"Oh, really now," said Tucker.

"Let me complete, please, Senator. Joseph Blackwood, after successfully cordoning off the *Apollo 11* landing and operational site, sent the rest of the crew, under the command of Jeremy Flockston, to visit the other *Apollo* landing sites and do the same cordoning-off job there."

"I want them all back at base in three days," demanded Tucker in gruff tones. "And I will be back to talk to all six of them."

"May I ask why you wish to speak to them?" said Maurice.

"I want to assess what they are doing at the base. I want to be sure they are contributing productively to the advancement of science and technology."

"Well, now, I can assure you, Senator, that they are not exactly having a seaside holiday on the moon. May I remind you that the 'maria' on the moon do not refer to seas as we know them here on Earth."

"I've managed to buy a bit of time with Tucker," said Maurice to Joseph and James during a televisual conference.

"You once dismissed my projects of preserving the original *Apollo* landing sites as mere sentimentalism. Perhaps they have a practical application after all!" said Joseph.

"Yes, I can use this to hold off Tucker for a few days."

"But we are in a real pickle regarding the televisual where Tucker wants all six of us together," said James.

"Harry, Margaret, and Rupert have come up with an ingenious plan. Here's Rupert to explain it," said Maurice.

"During his days at university, my nephew Harry experimented with ways to project live images from one place to another. Using his technique, we might be able to project Heather and Georgina onto the *Mars Endeavour* craft.

Maurice explained the situation to Heather and Georgina. The two ladies were taken to a small room. Equipment was set up and cameras trained on them.

"Just remember," said Gregory, "you are on the moon and in *Mars Endeavour*."

Three hundred yards away in another room, Maurice, Gregory, Rupert, Harry, and Margaret awaited the arrival of Tucker.

"Tucker is due here any moment," said Harry.

"Fingers crossed that this works," said Margaret rather nervously.

Five minutes later, Vincent Tucker was shown into the televisual conference room. Maurice and his companions held their breath. A sigh of relief came from them as before their eyes were the members of the *Mars Endeavour* crew, including Georgina and Heather.

"I want you to give an account of yourselves," said Tucker rather brusquely. "How have you been spending US taxpayers' money?"

Each crew member detailed the work they had been doing related to their own fields of specialization.

"And why have you spent so many man-hours in preserving the *Apollo* mission sites?" said Tucker.

"Harry Holbert and Margaret Woodford, NASAs two interns, have opened up a new branch of science called archaeoastronautics. While they have been the main thrust in this new science with their research into and reconstruction of the *Apollo* technology, we have extended that scientific practice to the moon by preserving for posterity the great achievements of the 1960s and early 1970s."

"Hmmmm," responded Tucker, clearly unimpressed. "The average American taxpayer is going to ask about the practical worth of all this."

"How do you know, Senator?" asked Georgina.

"Did you ask them all?" said Heather.

"I'm not too impressed by your snide questions," responded Tucker, now being put on the defensive. "My job is to ensure that the taxpayers get value for money."

"Could you come directly to the point, please, Senator?" said Maurice.

"A satellite paid for by Ore Mining Enterprises and developed by Planet Outreach made a number of orbits of the moon eighteen months ago and detected rich gold veins in the part of the Mare Tranquillitatis in which *Mars Endeavour* came down," Tucker explained.

"Yes, Senator, we know about this," said Joseph, "but how many times do we have to tell you that we can find no traces of gold in the region?"

"I need something of value there as I have to answer to the American taxpayers," protested Tucker.

"I think that what is more to the point, Senator, is that OME is going to have to answer to PO for the money it owes PO for that satellite. And both OME's and PO's respective boards of directors are going to have to give an account of this expenditure to their shareholders. Already OME and PO shares have lost 50 percent of their value on Wall Street."

Everyone wheeled round to see who the mysterious intruder was. It was Arthur Watern, director of the Marshall Space Flight Center.

"Watern!" said Tucker angrily. "What business is this of yours? Who invited you here?"

"It is very much my business," responded Arthur. "Planet Outreach was commissioned by the MSFC to develop a series of communication satellites to orbit the moon so as to strengthen communication between the Earth, the moon, and Mars. The money was not to be used for gold prospecting on the moon."

Tucker paced up and down the room, clearly thinking about how to respond.

"The space race is becoming increasingly expensive. We need to show the American taxpayers that it has some commercial worth. Over the last twenty years, there have been too many aborted missions to Mars and the other planets. Vast amounts of money have been spent on research and to no apparent practical end."

"That is not strictly true," said Maurice. "The 'aborted missions,' as you call them, were not aborted at all. They were designed to fly into the atmospheres of Jupiter and the other gas giants so as to determine their compositions. And we discovered a lot about the gas compositions of these planets as a result."

"And my own research into moon rock," said Jeremy, "has shown that bacteria frequently lands on the moon. This bacteria which thrives on radioactive rocks could do much in the way of developing future propulsion systems for spacecraft."

"How can bacteria survive in such a hostile environment such as is found on the moon?" argued Tucker.

"The bacteria is protected by a carbonaceous coating. When released from their shields and placed within radioactive compounds, the energy released by their digestion of these can act as the propulsion system for craft."

"It sounds rather far-fetched to me," said Tucker, shaking his head.

"No more far-fetched than your moon-gold," said Jeremy.

Tucker walked out in a bad-tempered huff-puff.

Once Tucker had left the base, Georgina and Heather came out of their confined space and joined the rest of the team. Arthur Watern was surprised to see them. Maurice explained the need for the secrecy and informed Arthur of the crisis situation currently developing.

"We have to hurry with the third *Saturn V* rocket," said Arthur. "How long will it take for completion?"

"Another three weeks?" said Harry.

"Look, Maurice," said Arthur, "if I send you about twenty people from my technical team, it could be completed in a week. Three weeks may be too late to save Joseph and Rodney."

"Well," Joseph said to James, "the latest lunar lander is waiting for us just four miles from here. As we agreed, you and Jeremy go next. I, as commander, and Rodney, as my second, will take the next one."

Five days later, Jeremy and James joined Heather and Georgina. All four were advised to stay on base and incognito until the return of Joseph and Rodney.

A week later and the third *Saturn V* rocket was ready for liftoff. About half an hour before the countdown, Rupert, ashen-faced, approached Maurice in the control room.

"Bad news," he said. "PO have launched their rocket. That was five hours ago. They have a good head start on us."

"How long will it take their rocket to reach the moon?"

"It is a faster traveling rocket than the old *Saturn V*. It will take just two and a half days."

Maurice got on the televisual immediately to Joseph and Rodney and told them the whole story.

"I think the best plan is to load up two lunar minibuses and drive about six miles from *Mars Endeavour*," said Joseph. "We should be able to load enough oxygen and supplies for three days. Rodney will drive one bus, and I will drive the other. Each bus can carry enough oxygen and supplies for two weeks, so it's not a problem."

Two days later, Joseph and Rodney left *Mars Endeavour* for the last time.

"It's sad to say goodbye to the old girl," said Joseph sadly.

"She's served us well over the past year," said Jeremy.

They drove their buses six miles across the mare. They would wait for the lunar lander that was programmed to land three miles further away. The lunar minibuses were made of the same tough plastic-type material that had been used to cordon off the *Apollo* landing sites. Although not cramped, they would be far from the comforts of the spacious city, which was *Mars Endeavour*.

Two days later, Joseph and Rodney waited with fear and expectation. Maurice told them by means of radio communication that it would happen in exactly one minute. One minute went by, and Joseph and Rodney were tense, silent, and fearful. But nothing happened. Five minutes went by—still nothing. Fifteen minutes—zero. The two men became more relaxed. All of a sudden, the sky near the horizon lit up. The otherwise jet-black lunar sky glowed with a brilliant white light. A mushroom cloud lifted itself gracefully into the sky and disappeared.

"Hello, Joseph, Rodney, are you there?" came Maurice's voice over the radio. "Are you both all right?"

"We are fine. We are OK," Joseph assured Maurice and the others who were with him. All cheered and clapped in joy and relief.

"Could you give a report on what you have seen?" Maurice asked.

"Yes," replied Joseph. "There appeared to be an explosion. An atomic explosion, we are sure, judging from the mushroom cloud which followed."

"Can you give us any kind of report on the condition of the *Mars Endeavour*?" Gregory asked.

"Give us a few minutes to exit the vehicle and set up some telescopic equipment?" said Rodney.

"I think the *Mars Endeavour* is still intact as the explosion occurred in a northerly direction. Judging from the level below the horizon from which it occurred, it seems as though the explosion was on the far side of the Moon," said Joseph.

"The far side of the moon?" exclaimed Harry.

"Yes," Joseph confirmed.

"Please use your telescopic equipment and home in on the craft and report to me on its current condition and status," said Maurice.

Twenty minutes later, Joseph and Rodney reentered the bus and reported back to Maurice and his team.

"We are more than overjoyed to say that *Mars Endeavour* is intact," said Joseph.

"That rocket sent by PO clearly missed its target," said Margaret.

"But how?" exclaimed Gregory. "Hitting a precise target on the moon is child's play these days," said Gregory. "And for technicians of the caliber at PO, this is astounding beyond words."

Rupert became very serious for a moment. "Listen to me. My friend in PO, the one who stayed on, knew what Tucker, OME, and PO were up to. He placed a robotic device in the engine and guided the rocket to crash on the far side of the moon."

"That's truly amazing," said Harry.

"But now he will need protection as PO et al will make a thorough investigation into the incident," said Maurice.

"He's safe enough," said Rupert. "My friend programmed the micro-robotic device to register the strike as having taken place in the part of the Mare Tranquillitatis on which *Mars Endeavour* is located."

"Let's see what Tucker's next move is, and we'll devise the rest of our strategy around that," said Rupert.

Joseph and Rodney drove back to *Mars Endeavour* and waited in better comfort for the lunar lander to arrive. Two days later, they said their second farewell to the "city" as they drove off to the capsule that would soon take them off the moon. During their final two days on *Mars Endeavour*, they equipped some robots with cameras and placed them around the craft's interior and exterior.

It was all over the media, *Mars Endeavour* had exploded in mysterious circumstances. The implications would be far-reaching for the future of space research and exploration. Sen. Vincent Tucker was being interviewed by a major US television network, CCN.

Interviewer: Senator Tucker, based upon the reports you have received from NASA, what do you think caused this explosion?

Tucker: We can never be sure, but it was most likely caused by a malfunction in one or more of the atomic-powered engines in the craft. We so much regret the loss of the crew. Our sincere condolences to their families.

Interviewer: What do you think this means for the future of space research?

Tucker: We do not contend, as some do, that space research should be halted and that we should simply concentrate on terrestrial issues, but we do think it needs to be restructured and reorientated?

Interviewer: Reorientated in what direction, Senator?

Tucker: In order to justify the vast amounts of taxpayers' money being funneled into NASA and its offshoots, space exploration should take on a more commercial aspect. Taxpayers need to see more tangible evidence for its benefits and more concrete returns on their money.

Interviewer: How precisely should this be done, Senator Tucker?

Tucker: By NASA, JPL, and MSFC working in greater collusion with private commercial space flight organizations.

Interviewer: At whose feet would you lay the blame for this appalling tragedy on the moon?

Tucker: At NASA's. Their safety standards are simply not up to scratch, and their funding must be reduced further. My committee will examine ways and means of diverting funds from NASA and toward private commercial space flight companies.

"So that's Tucker's way of obtaining public funds to pay for the PO satellite debacle," said Arthur to Maurice one day.

"The man is plainly a criminal and a fiend," responded Maurice.

"Anyway, when Joseph and Rodney return, we'll soon deal with Tucker."

Three days later, Joseph and Rodney arrived back on Earth. Maurice sent out a press statement that he was to call a major press conference in two days' time regarding *Mars Endeavour* and its crew.

"I don't see the purpose of your press conference, Cuthbertson," said Tucker to Maurice on the phone that morning. "Why do you want to call it? What can it profit anyone?"

"It's regarding the crew of the *Mars Endeavour*," said Maurice.

"They're all dead, man!" hollered Tucker. "What more can you tell the world? I hope your press conference is not designed to slag me and my STC off."

"It is only to give our condolences to the families of the crew members who perished in the *Mars Endeavour* explosion—we owe it to them. I will in no way criticize the STC or you, as I and NASA will take full responsibility for the *Mars Endeavour* failure."

"You stated in your brief calling for the press conference that you would have information of 'dramatic and momentous proportions.' What exactly do you mean by that?"

"I mean, after considering the investigative reports we have made into the catastrophe, we conclude that one possibility to account for the explosion was an experiment gone wrong with Heather Wilber's mini-LHC."

"All right, Cuthbertson, go ahead with your press conference, but you dare criticize the STC, you are going to have to answer for it big time to me."

Two days later, reporters from major TV and radio networks were gathered in the huge conference room at NASA HQ. The well-known reporters from the nation's largest newspapers were also assembled. They did not look too enthusiastic. Polls had shown that the general public had lost confidence in NASA, and on top of this, the press did not think that anything of any great moment would come from the administrator and his team.

"Ladies and gentlemen of the media," began Maurice Cuthbertson, "thank you all for coming here this evening. You are all aware of the publicity regarding the *Mars Endeavour* city craft and the drama connected to it over the last near eighteen months. So I won't go over that again. You are all already well-briefed on how events have unfolded since the crew left here."

"Have you nothing to say in the way of condolences to the families of the deceased crew members?" called out one reporter, interrupting Maurice's allocution.

"None whatsoever," replied Maurice. "It is the very last thing that is necessary. Condolences are not in order."

There were gasps of shock around the hall.

"First of all, I want you to look at the large screen behind me. We are going to see live footage of *Mars Endeavour* and its surroundings."

"You mean, what's left of it!" shouted out a reporter sarcastically.

The assembled reporters were then stunned to see a perfectly intact *Mars Endeavour*. One of the robots was equipped with a camera. By remote control from the conference room, the robot moved around the outside of the craft.

Inside the craft, other robots, which had been placed at various locations around the city, were switched on. The assembled reporters were treated to a tour of a perfectly intact *Mars Endeavour*.

"But what about the crew? Where are the crew? We don't see any of the crew," came the shouts from the press reporters.

"I'm coming to that in just a moment," said Maurice reassuringly. Maurice then pressed a button, and a door on the far right of the hall opened. In walked Joseph, Rodney, James, Jeremy, Georgina, and Heather. Following behind them were Gregory, Arthur, Rupert, Harry, Margaret, and Daniel North.

Maurice told the reporters everything from beginning to end.

CHAPTER
XI

PICKING UP THE PIECES

After his arrest, Vincent Tucker was indicted on numerous charges of fraud and embezzlement and one of attempted murder. Tucker was given fifty years in prison and his accomplices prison terms ranging between ten and forty years. OME and PO had their assets seized and put under the administration of NASA.

"I don't know if you guys are ready to go back into space again," said Maurice to Joseph and his crew.

"After the hell you've been through, I couldn't blame you for shunning the offer," said Gregory.

"We've discussed it, and we would be delighted to go back into space," replied Joseph.

Turning to Harry and Margaret, Maurice said, "You two have really earned your laurels. I want to offer you full-time employment with NASA. And if you young people would like a bit of adventure, you are more than welcome to train as astronauts."

"Well, regarding that," said Harry, "Margaret and I have something to tell you. Go on, Margaret."

"Harry and I are going to get married," said Margaret.

Everyone congratulated the two young interns.

"And we want to spend our honeymoon on *Mars Endeavour*," said Harry.

"And you can travel there on something safer and more comfortable than a *Saturn V* rocket," said Maurice. "With the additional assets from PO and OME, and the expertise from PO and NSH, we have developed craft that can fly directly to the moon from one of our space stations orbiting the Earth. Public confidence in the space program has been regained, so we are back into full swing with space research."

"One thing you two could do on the moon is to get *Mars Endeavour* shipshape for the planet it was destined to travel to," Rupert suggested.

"We have been giving some thought to *Mars Endeavour*," said Joseph. "Flying it on to Mars is one option, but we feel that its true home is on the moon. It has done such great work there."

"But it seems such a waste of resources in terms of money, technical expertise, and effort," said Maurice. "Here was a craft of the size of a small town that was meant to fly all the way to Mars to be the thrust for the building of even larger cities on the Red Planet, and all it managed to do was to get to the moon!"

"Looking back at it over the longer term," said Joseph, "and thinking of the future of space travel, the travail my crew and I went through may actually prove to have been a blessing in disguise."

Everyone looked at Joseph with countenances that displayed a mixture of shock and puzzlement.

"How is that, Joseph?" asked Gregory.

"Well, we have come to realize that sending humans to Mars is hazardous, regardless of the kind of chicanery and criminality practiced by Tucker and his ilk. Suppose something had gone wrong with *Mars Endeavour*, or any Mars-bound craft for that matter, halfway or thereabouts on its way to the Red Planet. There would have been no chance of rescue."

Maurice and Gregory both looked pensive. They realized this glaring defect in the whole space program.

"I would like Harry and Margaret to say something on this matter," continued Joseph.

"It is quite ironical," said Margaret, "that while our archeoastronautical endeavors were designed to effect a rescue mission, the original *Apollo* program had no provisions for the rescue of the astronauts in the event of failure. Yet it was this archaic technology which got Joseph and his crew off the moon!"

"We think that rescue should be a major component in any future program regarding space exploration," said Harry.

"So what exactly do you have in mind with regard to rescue operations in space?" Maurice asked.

"First of all, space travel will always carry with it a great deal of risk," said Harry. "But that risk can be minimized. *Mars Endeavour*, far from not living up to its name, is, in fact, the first step toward much safer journeys to Mars. It is the first component in a rescue structure, which we envisage as a tripartite system involving the Earth, the moon, and a relay station halfway between Mars and the Earth."

"Mining gold from the area in which *Mars Endeavour* came down," said Margaret, "would greatly help in the financial arrangements needed for such an ambitious project. Metals needed for the building of such craft can be mined and refined on the moon. Here is a chart showing the composition of the amount of metallic ore on the moon."

"The oxygen in the rock can be harnessed for human personnel," said Harry. "And Dr. Flockston's oxygen-producing plants can also provide much needed oxygen. Water molecules exist in the thin gases above the moon's surface and in reasonable abundance in permanently shadowed craters mainly at the lunar south pole. This map details these areas of water."

"This water can be piped to *Mars Endeavour* and any other base that may be built on the moon," said Margaret.

"Getting to and from the relay station and to and from Mars itself would be much easier than starting the journey from Earth," said Rodney.

"Also," said Heather, "what we learn from our experiences on the moon can be applicable to Mars. That can contribute to the greater success of future Mars missions."

"Basically, what we are saying is that Earth, the moon, Mars, and beyond into the more distant regions of the solar system is a seamless garment," said Georgina.

"The question now is as to how we handle the city we have already built on Mars," said Joseph.

"Until we have constructed the robotically-operated relay station, the robots on Mars can maintain the city there in its current condition," said Gregory. "They are not advanced enough to perform what you had originally been sent there to do, but they can prevent any deterioration in it."

"How long will it take to design and construct this relay station?" Maurice asked. "I reckon it would take about two years for the design stage and at least three years for the construction of it."

"We planned all that out during our time on *Mars Endeavour*," said Rodney.

"The design is almost complete. It just needs a few finishing touches," said Joseph. "The station itself could be constructed in Earth orbit in about three to three and a half years."

"And what about a manned mission to Mars?" asked Maurice.

"If there is any hurry to get there," said Rodney, "we could send *Mars Endeavour*—once the relay station is completed, of course."

"But then, while that would hasten on the Mars projects, it would leave a gap in the lunar side of the operation," said Maurice. "We would still have to construct a replacement for *Mars Endeavour*."

"I suggest," said Jeremy, "that we leave *Mars Endeavour* on the moon. We already know it is doing a fine job there."

"Are we all happy about that?" asked Maurice.

All heads nodded in agreement.

"Well," said Joseph, "Mars, here we come—but not quite yet."

AFTERWORD

TERRAFORMING

C an Mars ever be terraformed is a commonly asked question. The basic idea is to use giant orbiting mirrors to concentrate sunlight onto the planet's poles, melt the water there, and generally warm up the planet.

Water released from the poles would spread over the planet, thus allowing horticulture and agriculture to take place. The process of photosynthesis would create the necessary breathable gases for human habitation on the planet.

But it's not as easy as it often sounds. First of all, Mars has a little to no magnetic field. This, coupled with its low gravity, would cause the breathable gases (presuming these could be produced) to dissipate into space. Mars would simply resort to its original state.

There are a number of issues that future terraformers, such as our friends, Harry and Margaret et al, would have to consider if they set themselves the ambitious goal of making Mars less hostile to life. Mars has a more elliptical orbit around the sun than the Earth does, so there would be much greater differences in the climate of the two hemispheres, namely relatively cold southern winters and warm northern summers. Also, Mars is further from the sun, so there would be insufficient light for photosynthetic processes. Mars has less nitrogen than the Earth does, and nitrogen is essential for our atmosphere. There is an abundance of percholorates on the Martian surface, and these are poisonous to human life. And as Mars is nearer the asteroid belt than is the Earth, there would be a greater chance of Mars experiencing a meteorite impact.

What about domes?

Provided a proper supply chain between Earth and Mars could be established and a near self-sufficiency in food and oxygen-producing substances could be achieved, the type of structures invented by the NASA team in the story would have to be constructed. Under these greenhouse conditions, humans could live quite comfortably on Mars.

Is there any life on Mars now?

The evidence garnered from various unmanned craft sent to Mars shows that billions of years ago, Mars was more Earth-like and more suited for life to evolve. That is not the case now. Mars's thin atmosphere, low gravity, and weak magnetic field means that the planet has no shield against radiation from outer space. Therefore, complex forms of life above the bacterial level are unlikely to exist. Perhaps the best place to look for life on Mars would be under the planet's surface. Core samples taken at subterranean levels may yield positive results in terms of any biological activity on Mars.

What are the chances of the kind of science-fiction technology depicted in this story ever becoming science fact?

In terms of the current pace of technological development, the chances of this kind of technological sophistication being developed in the timeframe mentioned in the story (2054) seems unlikely. Yet science can be full of surprises. In 1950, the late Sir Fred Hoyle thought that sending rockets into Earth orbit would not be possible for another hundred years from then. Not only were rockets sent into space, but also man landed on the moon in 1969—only nineteen years later.

It is reasonable to predict that at some time within the next hundred years, structures like the ones described in the story will be built on the moon and Mars. Technology is advancing with ever-increasing rates of rapidity, so the structures and events described in the story may not be too far off center. It is surely only a question of "when," not "if."